The Lion and the Mouse

ADAPTED BY
Teresa Mlawer

ILLUSTRATED BY
Olga Cuéllar

chosen spot
publishing

Once upon a time, there was a little mouse that lived happily in the jungle.

He loved to explore as he collected sweet fruits to eat.

One day, the little mouse was strolling through the jungle. Searching for a shady place to rest, he went deeper and deeper into the jungle.

Suddenly, he spotted something in the distance:
a huge lion was sleeping under the shadow of a big tree!

Since the lion was fast asleep, the little mouse decided to check out the so-called "King of the Jungle."

He carefully climbed onto the lion's tail and started running across his back.

He reached the lion's head and inspected his mane and ears, and gently pulled his whiskers.

With the lion still sleeping, the mouse even lifted one of the lion's eyelids to find out the color of his eyes.

Precisely at that moment, the lion woke up with a jolt.
He gave a loud roar and shook his head from side to side.

The frightened little mouse dropped to the ground,
but the lion quickly caught him between his claws.

Lifting the little mouse to get a better look at him, the lion said, "How dare you wake me up? I'm going to eat you right now."

"Please don't eat me," cried the frightened little mouse. "Please forgive me, King of the Jungle. If you let me go, I'll never forget it. Maybe one day I can repay your kindness and be of help to you!"

Upon hearing this, the lion roared with laughter and said, "Well, that's silly! How could a tiny mouse like you possibly help a mighty lion like me?

I'm the biggest and strongest animal in the jungle, and you're just a small, defenseless creature! What could you ever do to help me?"

"You never know," replied the little mouse. "Size and strength are not everything. I can only promise that if you let me go, I will never ever forget it."

Considering what the mouse had said, the lion picked him up and studied him carefully. With a smile, the lion set him free, and the grateful mouse scurried away.

A few weeks later, the mouse was walking in the jungle when he heard a terrible sound: Rawrrr! Rawrrr! Rawrrr!

He recognized the roar, and immediately ran in the direction of the noise.

He arrived to find the poor lion caught in a net, unable to move. He had fallen into a trap set by some hunters who wanted to capture him.

As soon as the lion saw the mouse, he let out another sad roar. He tried with all his strength to free himself from the net, but he couldn't. He was trapped!

"My dear friend," said the mouse. "Don't worry. I'll help you."

"How can you help me?" asked the lion. "I'm caught in this net and the hunters will be here soon."

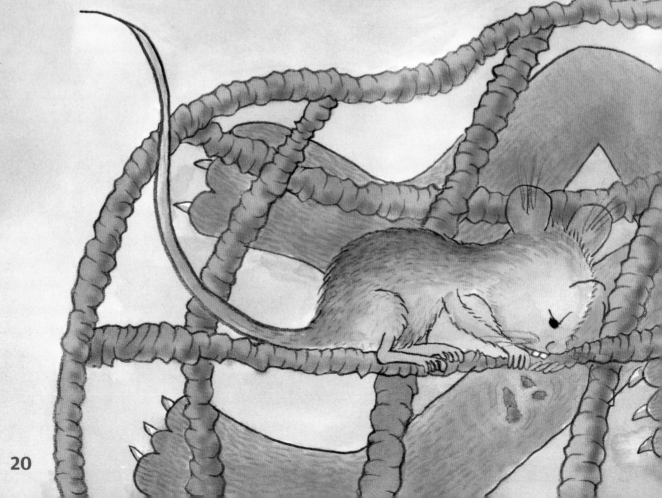

"Have faith," said the mouse, as he began to nibble on the rope that was trapping his friend.

The little mouse nibbled at the rope nonstop. Finally, he managed to make a hole in the net big enough for the lion to escape!

"I don't know how to thank you," said the lion. "You saved my life."

"You don't need to thank me," said the little mouse. "You spared my life once. Now it's my turn to pay you back."

"Thanks to you," said the lion, "I've learned that it's important to keep a promise, and that even a small friend can be a big help."

What lesson have we learned from this fable?

Even a small friend can be a big help.

FOR INFORMATION, PLEASE CONTACT CHOSEN SPOT PUBLISHING, P.O. BOX 266, CANANDAIGUA, NEW YORK, 14424

ISBN 978-0-9864313-5-7   10 9 8 7 6 5 4 3 2 1   PRINTED IN CHINA